For Every Child, A Better World

"When I was young, my ambition was to be one of the people who makes a difference in this world. My hope still is to leave this world a little better for my being here."

— **Jim Henson**

Dear Reader:

Today many people in the world are facing great difficulties. Many of them are hungry. Many of them have no homes. Many of them cannot read or write. Many of them are at war.

Many of them are children.

It was my father's dream to make the world a better place for children everywhere. *For Every Child, A Better World* is one of the ways in which we are keeping this dream alive. It is a challenging and provocative book. It is also a hopeful one, allowing parents to show their children how some people are working to make this a better world for all of us.

Children who begin to think about others with understanding and compassion grow up to be understanding and compassionate adults. We believe this book can help children become the kind of adults who will make the world a better place.

Sincerely,

Brian Henson

This book is dedicated
to the memory of Audrey Hepburn.

To the children of the world.
— Kermit

To my sisters, Ellen and June.
— Bruce McNally

For Every Child, A Better World

by Kermit the Frog

in cooperation with the United Nations

as told to Louise Gikow and Ellen Weiss
illustrated by Bruce McNally

A portion of the proceeds from the sale of this book
will be used to support United Nations projects.

A MUPPET PRESS/GOLDEN BOOK

Every child needs food to eat.

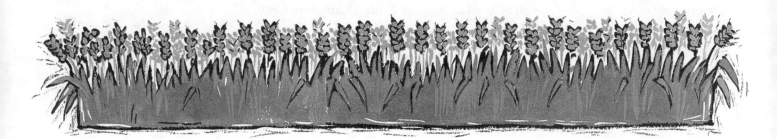

But sometimes there isn't enough to go around.

Every child needs clean water to drink.

But sometimes you have to go a long way to get it.

Every child needs a home.

But some children don't have one.

Every child needs clean air to breathe.

But sometimes it's dirty.

Every sick child needs to be able to get medicine.

But sometimes there isn't any.

Every child needs to have the chance to go to school.

But sometimes there are no books or teachers.

Every child needs to play.

But some children have to work.

Every child needs peace.

But sometimes there is war.

Every child needs to be able to decide
what to think and feel and believe.

But some children are not allowed.

All over the world, people are working to see that every child gets what every child needs. This will mean a better world for all of us.

And every child needs a better world.

Following are just a few of the members of the United Nations family working hard to make this a better world. Doctors, teachers, nurses, engineers, and scientists are among the many dedicated people employed by these agencies and programs.

Food and Agriculture Organization
The FAO works to help all people have enough healthy food to eat.

International Fund for Agricultural Development
The IFAD tries to make sure that all nations can afford to grow enough food to feed all their people.

World Meteorological Organization
The WMO gives accurate information about the weather, climate, and environment to people around the world.

United Nations Industrial Development Organization
The UNIDO helps countries build modern factories and machinery to make things their people need.

United Nations Development Program
The UNDP helps countries develop their natural and human resources.

World Health Organization
The WHO works to keep all the people of the world healthy.

International Labour Organization
The ILO tries to make sure that working people everywhere are treated fairly.

United Nations Educational, Scientific, and Cultural Organization

The UNESCO helps countries cooperate, using education, science, culture, and communication to make the world a safer and more peaceful place.

World Intellectual Property Organization

When someone invents something or writes a book or a piece of music or a film script, the WIPO helps make sure that all people respect the creator's right to be rewarded for his or her work.

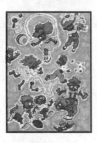

UNICEF

UNICEF (the United Nations Children's Fund) is a United Nations program that helps children all over the world to live happy and healthy lives.

General Agreement on Tariffs and Trade
The basic aim of GATT is to make it easier for countries to trade with each other.

International Atomic Energy Agency
The IAEA helps nations safely develop and use atomic energy for peaceful purposes.

International Civil Aviation Organization
The ICAO helps people all over the world travel safely by air.

International Maritime Organization
The IMO makes it easier to send things all over the world by ship.

International Monetary Fund
The IMF helps nations cooperate on money matters.

International Telecommunication Union
The ITU works to improve telephone, radio, and television service for people around the world.

Universal Postal Union
The UPU helps mail travel from country to country.

World Bank
The World Bank is actually made up of three organizations. Together they provide loans from countries that have money to spare to countries that are less well-off. This helps the less fortunate countries improve living conditions for their people.

For more information about the United Nations and its agencies, contact the Public Inquiries Unit, United Nations Headquarters, New York, NY 10017 Telephone: (212) 963-4475.